THE ASTC

THE
ASTONISHED HEART

A Play in Six Scenes

by
NOEL COWARD

From
TONIGHT AT 8:30

SAMUEL FRENCH, INC.
45 WEST 25TH STREET   NEW YORK 10010
7623 SUNSET BOULEVARD HOLLYWOOD 90046
LONDON   TORONTO

THE ASTONISHED HEART

Produced by John C. Wilson at the National Theatre in New York City on November 24, 1936, as one of a series of nine one-act plays by Noel Coward, under the title of "TO-NIGHT AT EIGHT-THIRTY." The play was directed by the author and the cast was as follows:

CHRISTIAN FABER	*Noel Coward.*
BARBARA (His Wife) . . .	*Joyce Carey.*
LEONORA VAIL	*Gertrude Lawrence.*
SUSAN BIRCH	*Joan Swinstead.*
TIM VERNEY	*Anthony Pelissier.*
ERNEST	*Edward Underdown.*
SIR REGINALD FRENCH . . .	*Alan Webb.*

The action of the entire play takes place in the drawing-room of the Fabers' flat in London.

SCENE I.—Late afternoon, November 1935.

SCENE II.—Late afternoon. November 1934.

SCENE III.—Midnight. January 1935.

SCENE IV.—Dawn. April 1935.

SCENE V.—Evening. November 1935.

SCENE VI.—Late afternoon. November 1935.

CHARACTERS

Produced at the Phœnix Theatre, Charing Cross Road, London, W.C.2, in January, 1936, with the following cast of Characters :

CHRISTIAN FABER	. . . .	*Noel Coward.*
BARBARA (his Wife)	. . . .	*Alison Leggatt.*
LEONORA VAIL	. . . .	*Gertrude Lawrence.*
TIM VERNEY	. . . .	*Anthony Pelissier.*
SUSAN BIRCH	. . . .	*Everley Gregg.*
SIR REGINALD FRENCH	. . .	*Alan Webb.*
ERNEST	. . . . .	*Edward Underdown.*

The action of the entire play takes place in the drawing-room of the Fabers' flat in London.

SCENE I.—Late afternoon. November 1935.

SCENE II.—Late afternoon. November 1934.

SCENE III.—Midnight. January 1935.

SCENE IV.—Dawn. April 1935.

SCENE V.—Evening. November 1935.

SCENE VI.—Late afternoon. November 1935.

THE ASTONISHED HEART

SCENE I

The action of the entire play takes place in the drawing-room of the FABERS' *flat in London. The flat is on the top floor of one of the newly-erected apartment buildings in the region of Hyde Park. The furniture is comfortable and good without conceding too much to prevailing fashion. On the* R. *double doors lead to the hall, dining-room and* BARBARA'S *bedroom and bathroom, etc. On the* L. *other double doors lead to* CHRISTIAN'S *part of the flat, his bedroom, consulting-room and office.*

When the CURTAIN *rises it is late afternoon in November 1935. The lights are on, but the curtains have not been drawn and* BARBARA *is standing looking out of the window into the foggy dusk. She is a tranquil, intelligent woman of about thirty-six or seven. Her back is to the room and she is drumming her fingers on the window-pane.* SUSAN BIRCH *is seated on the sofa with her hands clasped on her lap. Her age is somewhere between thirty and forty and she is plainly and efficiently dressed as befits a secretary. She is sitting very still, although occasionally she bites her lip nervously.* TIM VERNEY, *a nice-looking man in the early thirties, is standing in front of the fireplace on the* L. *smoking a cigarette. There is an air of strain in the room as though any one of them might cry out at any moment. The silence is broken by* BARBARA.

BARBARA (*up* R.C.). It looks terribly dreary out, but it's like that anyhow at this time of year, isn't it !

TIM (*at the fire*). Yes.

BARBARA. The traffic seems slower than usual—1 expect that's my imagination.

TIM. Don't you think you'd better come away from the window now ?

BARBARA. Yes, I suppose I had.

(*She comes slowly down and sits on the sofa next to* SUSAN, L. *of her.*)

Don't worry, Tim, about the window I mean, it's something we've got to get used to like everything else—part of the whole thing.

TIM. Yes, I know.

BARBARA (*to* SUSAN). She answered the telephone herself, didn't she ?

SUSAN (*with an effort*). Yes.

BARBARA. She ought to be here by now.

SUSAN (*looking at her wrist-watch*). Yes—yes, she ought.

BARBARA. I suppose Ernest would be shocked if we had a cocktail, wouldn't he ?

TIM. That doesn't matter.

BARBARA (*almost irritably*). I know it doesn't matter, Tim, I was only thinking how funny it is that whether Ernest should be shocked or not shocked should come into my mind at all—will you ring for him ?

TIM. All right. (*He rings the bell by the fireplace.*)

BARBARA. I expect you think I'm talking too much.

SUSAN (*trying to smile*). No, I don't, dear.

BARBARA. Talking's useful, it makes a little noise, but not too much, just enough to distract the attention——

SUSAN. I know. (*She gets up and begins to move up stage.*)

BARBARA. What is it ?

SUSAN. I thought perhaps I'd better go into the office.

BARBARA (*moving to* R. *end of the sofa*). No, don't, sit down again, stay with us.

SUSAN (*coming down* C.). Very well. (*She sits down again, at* L. *end of the sofa.*)

(ERNEST, *the butler, enters* R.)

ERNEST. You rang, madame ?

BARBARA. Make a cocktail, will you, Ernest, a Dry Martini I think, don't you, Tim ?

TIM (*absently*). Yes, a Dry Martini.

ERNEST. Very good, madame.

BARBARA. When Mrs. Vail arrives—I'm—I'm expecting her—— (*Her voice breaks slightly.*)

ERNEST. Yes, madame.

(*He goes out* R.)

BARBARA. That was silly of me, wasn't it ?—Unnecessary—he knew perfectly well we were expecting her——

TIM. She's probably held up in the traffic.

BARBARA. Yes, it's bad at this time of day—I'd like a cigarette, Susan, there's a box just by you.

(SUSAN *silently hands her the box and she takes a cigarette and lights it.*)

TIM. Poor woman.

BARBARA. Leonora ? Yes—it's awful for her.

SUSAN (*bitterly*). She'll get over it.

BARBARA. So shall we, I expect—in time.

SUSAN. It doesn't matter to her, not really, not like it matters to us—she'll cry a lot and be beautifully heartbroken——

BARBARA. Don't be unkind.

SUSAN (*violently*). I hate her.

BARBARA (*turning away*). Oh, don't, Susan—what's the use of that——

SUSAN. I don't care whether it's any use or not—I hate her, more than I've ever hated anyone in my whole life——

BARBARA. You might just as well hate a piece of notepaper because someone's written something cruel on it.

(SIR REGINALD FRENCH *comes through the double doors up* L. *He is an authoritative, elderly surgeon.*)

SIR REGINALD.   She hasn't arrived yet ?   (*He comes a little way into the room.*)

(BARBARA *rises and faces up to him.*)

TIM.   She's on her way.

SIR REGINALD.   Good.

BARBARA.   There isn't much time, is there ?

SIR REGINALD (*gently*).   No, I'm afraid not.   (*He turns to go again.*)

BARBARA.   Is he—conscious ?

SIR REGINALD.   Only for a brief moment, every now and then.

BARBARA.   It's then that he asks for her ?   In those brief moments ?

SIR REGINALD.   Yes.

BARBARA.   I'll send her straight in when she comes. (*She sits again.*)

SIR REGINALD.   Do, my dear.

(*He goes out.*)

SUSAN.   Oh God !

(*She breaks down and cries softly.* BARBARA *puts an arm round her.*)

TIM.   Shut up, Susan.

SUSAN.   I can't help it—it would have been much better if only you'd let me go into the office when I wanted to.

BARBARA.   I'd rather you cried here with us than all by yourself in there.

(*There is a pause.*)

SUSAN (*dabbing her eyes*).   I'm all right now.

BARBARA.   Don't make too much of an effort, Susan, it's a dreadful strain—I'd cry if I could—tears are a little relief—they let the grief out for a minute or two —I envy them——

(ERNEST *enters with a tray on which is a cocktail-shaker and four glasses.*)

Put them on the small table, Ernest—thank you, Ernest.

(ERNEST *puts down the tray on the table* L. *by the fire and goes out.* TIM *takes a cocktail to* SUSAN *and* BARBARA *and then one for himself.*)

TIM (*drinking*). He's certainly made it dry enough.
BARBARA (*sipping hers and smiling faintly*). Strong enough too—oh dear——

(*There is the sound of the front-door bell. They all jump slightly.*)

TIM. Here she is—at last——
BARBARA (*suddenly*). How extraordinary—d'you see what I mean ? (*She rises, moves down and turns up.*) It's the same, exactly the same as a year ago—you were there, Tim, just where you are now, with a cocktail glass in your hand—you were there, Susan, only you had your glasses on and a packet of papers in your lap—don't you remember—the first time she ever came into this room—— ?

(ERNEST *opens the door and announces :* " **Mrs. Vail** " *as the lights fade.*)

SCENE II

When the lights come up on the scene, BARBARA, TIM, SUSAN *and* ERNEST *are all in the same positions as the preceding scene.* SUSAN *is wearing glasses and has a packet of papers in her lap, her jumper is blue instead of grey.* BARBARA *is wearing a tea gown.* TIM *is in the same suit.*

ERNEST (*announcing*). Mrs. Vail.

(LEONORA VAIL *enters. She is a lovely creature of about thirty, exquisitely dressed and with great charm of manner.*)

BARBARA (*greeting her*). My dear—after all these years——

(*They meet* C.)

LEONORA. Isn't it lovely ?

(*They kiss affectionately.*)

BARBARA. Bring some fresh cocktails, Ernest.
ERNEST. Yes, madame.

(*He goes out.*)

BARBARA (*introducing her*). This is Susan Birch, Chris's right hand.

(LEONORA *shakes hands with* SUSAN.)

And this is Tim Verney, Chris's left hand—or perhaps it's the other way round—settle it among yourselves —Leonora Vail—Ames that was——

(*They " How do you do."*)

LEONORA. Leonora Ames, terrible at games ! Do you remember ?
BARBARA. Of course I do.

(*They both laugh.*)

LEONORA (*shaking hands with* TIM). I think Barbara wrote that beastly little rhyme herself.
TIM (*smiling*). Was it true ?
LEONORA. Absolutely.
BARBARA. I can't possibly say you haven't changed, you've changed more thoroughly than anyone I have ever seen.
LEONORA. Having our hair up makes a great difference.

(TIM *pours out a cocktail.*)

BARBARA. Your voice has changed too, but I recognized it on the telephone.

LEONORA. I'd have known yours anywhere.

TIM. Have a cocktail, it's mostly water now—perhaps you'd rather wait for a fresh one.

LEONORA (*taking it*). That'll do beautifully. (*She holds it up towards* BARBARA.) The nastiest girl in the school. (*She is down stage* L.C., *her back to the audience.*)

BARBARA (*laughing*). But the best King Lear.

LEONORA (*also laughing*). Oh, of course—I'd forgotten that.

BARBARA. I foresee a flood of reminiscence.

TIM (*making a movement to go up to the doors* L.). So do I—come along, Susan, we'd better go.

BARBARA. No, don't go—you can bear it, Tim, you'll probably discover a lot of useful little psychological echoes from my childhood——

SUSAN (*rising*). I must go anyhow—all these have to be dealt with. (*She indicates the papers in her hand.*)

TIM. Is there a patient in there now ?

SUSAN (*glancing at her watch as she moves up* R. *of the sofa*). Yes, but her time's nearly up.

LEONORA (*at the fire, putting her glass down—to* BARBARA). Does he work all day long, your husband ?

BARBARA. Yes, most of the night as well sometimes.

LEONORA. What's he like ?

BARBARA. Horrible.

LEONORA. I sympathize, mine was an absolute darling, so much so that I divorced him after eighteen months——

SUSAN. Good-bye, Mrs. Vail.

(*She exits up* L.)

LEONORA. Good-bye.

TIM. We shall probably meet again very soon.

LEONORA. I hope so.

BARBARA. Ask Chris to come in for a second if he can when he's got rid of his patient.

TIM. All right.

(*He goes out.*)

LEONORA.   What a nice man. (*At the fire, looks at herself in the mirror.*)

BARBARA.   Tim's a dear, he's extremely brilliant too ; Chris thinks the world of him. (*She gets the cigarette-box from the table* L. *of the sofa.*)

LEONORA.   He must be wonderful. (*She crosses to the sofa.*)

BARBARA.   Who, Chris ?

(*She hands her a cigarette.*)

LEONORA.   Yes, a little frightening, though, I should think.

BARBARA (*sitting at* R. *end of the sofa and smiling*). Oh no, he's not in the least frightening—he gets a bit abstracted every now and then—when he's working too hard.

LEONORA (*sitting at* L. *end of the sofa*).   Dear Barbara, how nice this is—how long ago is it ?

BARBARA.   Seventeen — no eighteen years — I'm thirty-five now, I left long before you did——

LEONORA.   I remember missing you dreadfully.

BARBARA.   It was after the War when you went to America ?   (*She lights her cigarette.*)

LEONORA.   Yes, just after.   Father left Brazil in 1918 and at the beginning of 1919 we went to Washington.

BARBARA.   When were you married ?

LEONORA.   Oh, a long while after, several years.

BARBARA.   Was he really such a—a darling ?

LEONORA.   Oh, it was all horrid.   He was much older than me, very rich—fortunately—that's all there was to it really.

BARBARA.   And you never wanted to marry again ?

LEONORA.   I wanted to once, but it wasn't possible, everything went wrong——

(ERNEST *comes in with fresh cocktails, and crosses in front of the sofa to the cocktail table.*)

BARBARA.   I'm so sorry.

LEONORA.   I minded horribly at the time, but I

travelled a bit and got over it, it's a long while ago anyhow.

BARBARA. How long have you been in England ?

LEONORA. Only two weeks—I've got a darling little house, only rented of course. When will you come and dine ?

BARBARA. Whenever you like.

LEONORA. And your husband, Chris ?

BARBARA. I'm sure he'd love to, but it all depends, you can never count on him——

LEONORA. I'm longing to see him.

(ERNEST, *having deposited the cocktail-shaker on the tray, goes out, taking with him the empty one.*)

BARBARA. He'll probably come in soon for a moment.

LEONORA. Is it never more than a moment ?

BARBARA. Oh, yes—not quite as bad as that—but being married to eminence requires a little forbearance, especially if the eminence is dear to you. (*She rises and crosses to the cocktail table.*)

LEONORA (*moving to R. end of the sofa*). No holidays ?

BARBARA. Yes—last year we got a full month— we went to Italy, Como first and then down to Venice, it was lovely. He got a bit restive during the last week, but I persuaded him to stay the course.

LEONORA. I should be jealous, I think.

BARBARA. Jealous ?

LEONORA. But you're better balanced than I am —less emotional—you always were——

BARBARA (*bringing a cocktail to* LEONORA). It would be tiresome to go on being emotional after twelve years of marriage. (*She gives her the cocktail.*)

LEONORA. I don't really want another.

BARBARA. Come on—one more—I will too.

LEONORA. All right. (*She drinks.*) What does he do exactly ?

BARBARA (*gently*). He's only one of the most famous psychiatrists in the world, dear. (*She sits at L. end of the sofa.*)

LEONORA (*laughing*). I know that—be patient with

me—psychiatrist is only a word to me—it's nothing to do with bone-setting, is it ?

BARBARA (*laughing too*). No, nothing whatever— you're thinking of osteopathy——

LEONORA. No, I'm not, it's something like psychiatrist—another word.

BARBARA. Chiropracter.

LEONORA. That's it.

BARBARA. You'd better not mention that to Chris, he doesn't approve of chiropracters at all——

LEONORA. What's a psychiatrist then ?

BARBARA. Someone who cures diseases of the mind——

LEONORA. Oh, repressions and inhibitions and all that sort of thing.

BARBARA. Yes, all that sort of thing.

LEONORA. How exciting.

BARBARA. Yes, more interesting than exciting.

LEONORA. You have a superior look in your eye, Barbara, and I resent it deeply.

BARBARA. I'm sorry, dear.

LEONORA. I know I'm idiotic really, but it's most tactless of you to remind me of it. How does he start his treatments ? Just a series of embarrassing questions ?

BARBARA. Frightfully embarrassing.

LEONORA. I've read about it in books. You have to remember sinister little episodes of your childhood —falling in love with the cook—or being frightened by a goat—then you have to determine the cook or sublimate the goat or something, and you go away completely cured and sleep like a top.

BARBARA. I see that your ignorance was only an affectation, you have the whole thing in a nutshell.

LEONORA. It must be fascinating work, unearthing everybody's rattling little skeletons and fitting them together like Meccano. What about himself ?

BARBARA. How do you mean ?

LEONORA. Does he know all about himself right

from the beginning ?   Is everything cut and dried and accounted for ?

BARBARA.   I expect so.

LEONORA.   And you ?   Has he a chart of you hanging up over his desk ?

BARBARA.   He doesn't need a chart of me, Leonora.

LEONORA.   Something in your manner tells me that I've gone too far—— Oh dear—I didn't mean to—don't be cross.

BARBARA (*smiling*).   I'm not in the least cross.

LEONORA.   I suppose he'd know all about me in a minute, wouldn't he ?   The very first second he clapped eyes on me.

BARBARA.   Certainly.

LEONORA.   How terrifying.

BARBARA.   Don't pretend, Leonora, I'm perfectly sure you're not terrified of anyone.

LEONORA.   Do his patients fall in love with him ?

BARBARA.   Practically always.

LEONORA.   Don't you hate that ?

BARBARA.   You are funny, Leonora.

LEONORA.   Am I ?   Nicely funny or nastily funny ?

BARBARA.   Charmingly funny.

LEONORA (*rises and moves down stage, looking at the room*).   Oh dear, I can't wait to see him, do tell someone to hurry him up, I shall have to go in a minute. He hasn't got a moustache, has he ?   (*She goes to the cocktail table and puts down her glass.*)

BARBARA.   No.

LEONORA.   Beard ?

BARBARA.   No beard.

LEONORA.   Tall or short ?

BARBARA.   Short.

LEONORA.   Fat ?

BARBARA.   Not exactly fat, let's say a little podgy.

LEONORA.   Oh, Barbara !

BARBARA.   He has very little chance of getting exercise, you see ; still, he does his best with those things in the bathroom——

LEONORA (*horrified*). What things ? (*Leaning on the back of the upstage armchair* L.)

BARBARA. You know, they're attached to the wall and you gasp and strain and they snap back again—he has a rowing machine too.

LEONORA. I know, I've seen them in gymnasiums on ships.

BARBARA. He finds it very effective.

LEONORA. You're lying, aren't you ?

BARBARA. Yes, Leonora.

LEONORA. I suppose he's eight feet high and absolutely bewitching.

BARBARA. If you care for long black moustaches, yes.

LEONORA. I've made up my mind to fall in love with him on sight.

BARBARA. He's quite used to that.

LEONORA (*sits on the arm of the upstage armchair*). You're positively smug about him, Barbara—tell me seriously—do you really adore him ?

BARBARA. I love him very much.

LEONORA. How marvellous. And does he love you ?

BARBARA. Really, Leonora !

LEONORA (*rising*). I know I'm behaving badly, do forgive me—— (*At the fire.*) Darling, I think I'd like just another little sip if there's any more in the shaker——

BARBARA (*rising*). It's practically full—— (*She crosses to the cocktail table.*)

(BARBARA *re-fills her glass.* CHRISTIAN FABER *comes into the room from the door up* L. *He is about forty years old, tall and thin. He moves quickly and decisively as though there was never quite enough time for all he had to do.*)

LEONORA. At last ! (*She gets down stage by the fireplace, facing up stage.*)

CHRISTIAN (*surprised*). What ? (*He gets to* L.C.)

BARBARA. This is Mrs. Vail, Chris, one of my oldest friends. We were at school together——

CHRISTIAN (*absently*). Oh—how do you do. (*He goes and shakes hands.*)

BARBARA.   Cocktail ?

CHRISTIAN.   No, I've got some more work to do.
(*He moves up to* BARBARA.)

LEONORA.   I think it only fair that you should know
that until Barbara disillusioned me I thought that you
were a chiropracter.

CHRISTIAN (*smiling perfunctorily*).   Did you really ?
(*To* BARBARA.)   Listen, dear, we are dining with Mary
to-night, aren't we ?

BARBARA.   Yes.

CHRISTIAN.   Well, you go without me and tell her I'll
come in for coffee——

BARBARA (*laughing*).   She knows that already, darling,
she told me on the telephone this morning.

CHRISTIAN (*with a smile*).   Mary is one of the most
intelligent women I know.

LEONORA (*with slightly forced impudence*).   I also
thought you had a long moustache !

CHRISTIAN (*not quite understanding*).   What—— ?

BARBARA (*quickly*).   Moustache, dear, Leonora thought
you had a moustache.

CHRISTIAN (*with a completely empty smile*).   No—I
haven't a moustache.

(*He bows politely and goes out up* L.)

LEONORA.   I'd rather he was a chiropracter.   (*She
crosses back to the sofa.*)

BARBARA.   Never mind.

LEONORA (*below* R. *end of sofa*).   He didn't even see
me, I do think it's a shame.

BARBARA (*at* L. *end of sofa*).   He saw you all right.

LEONORA.   You're being superior again, it's odious of
you.

BARBARA.   When do you want us to come and
dine ?

LEONORA.   I shan't even ask him, I like the other
young man much better, Tim whatever his name was,
bring him instead—next Wednesday ?

BARBARA (*going behind the desk to get her book from it*).
Wait a minute.

LEONORA (R. *of the desk*). Do you want to go to a play or just sit and talk ?

BARBARA. I don't mind a bit, whichever you like— but I'd rather make it Thursday.

LEONORA. All right—Thursday—we'll decide whether to go out or not later. (*Putting on her gloves.*)

BARBARA. That'll be lovely.

LEONORA. I really must go now——

BARBARA. You're sure you wouldn't like to stay and have your bones set or anything ?

LEONORA. No, I've given up the whole idea.

BARBARA. What whole idea ?

LEONORA. About falling madly in love with your husband and him falling madly in love with me and then me having a lovely " old friends together " scene with you and everyone behaving beautifully and making sacrifices all round——

BARBARA. What's your telephone number ?

LEONORA. You're not going to put me off, are you ?

BARBARA. Don't be so silly, of course not.

LEONORA. Kensington three-three-eight-two.

BARBARA (*scribbling it down*). Kensington three-three-eight-two.

LEONORA. I'll expect you on Thursday—about eight ?

BARBARA. Do you really want me to ask Tim ?

LEONORA. Of course, he's an angel, and bring your old chiropodist too if he'll come—— (*Going to the door.*)

BARBARA (*laughingly, as they go out*). I'll try to persuade him——

(*Their voices are heard talking and laughing in the hall.* TIM *comes in up* L. *and goes over to the desk. He rummages about on it.* BARBARA *returns.*)

Oh, Tim, you made me jump. What are you doing ?

TIM. Is there a Bible in the house ?

BARBARA (*coming to* R. *of desk*). I suppose there must be somewhere. Whatever do you want it for ?

TIM. Chris wants a quotation to use in his lecture on Friday——

BARBARA. Does he know a special one—— ?

Tim.   Vaguely—something in Deuteronomy——

(Ernest *enters* R.)

Barbara.   Oh, Ernest, is there a Bible in the house ?
Ernest.   I think the cook has one, madame.
Barbara.   Ask her if she'll lend it to me for a minute,
will you ?
Ernest.   Very good, madame.

(*He goes out.*)

Barbara (*crossing* L.).   Isn't she lovely ?
Tim.   Who ?   The cook ?
Barbara.   No, don't be so silly, Leonora.
Tim.   Very smooth and shiny.   (*He sits on the* L. *edge
of the desk.*)
Barbara.   Didn't you like her ?
Tim.   Yes, I suppose so, I only saw her for a moment.
Barbara.   She fell in love with you at first sight.
She wants you to dine with her on Thursday.
Tim.   Good God !
Barbara.   It's all right, I shall be there to protect
you.
Tim.   I hate dinner-parties.
Barbara.   You mustn't be disagreeable.

(Ernest *re-enters with a Bible.*)

(*Crossing* C.)   Ah, thank you, Ernest.
Ernest.   Have you finished with the cocktail things,
madame ?
Barbara.   Yes, thank you.

(Ernest *takes the cocktail tray away behind the desk
as* Susan *enters up* L.   Susan *comes to* L. *of* Barbara
and Tim *to* R. *of* Barbara, *down stage* C.)

Susan.   Did you find one ?
Tim.   Yes, it's the cook's.
Susan.   It's Moses, Deuteronomy twenty something
——   It starts with " The Lord shall smite thee——"

(*They look through the Bible together.*)

(*To* BARBARA.)   It's for his paper on the Development of Psychopathology starting with Hippocrates——

TIM.   This must be it——   (*He reads.*)   " The Lord shall smite thee with madness, and blindness, and astonishment of the heart."

SUSAN.   Yes, that's it.

(*She takes the Bible and goes off as the lights fade.*)

SCENE III

When the lights come up on the scene, CHRISTIAN *and* LEONORA *are discovered standing by the fireplace, his arms are round her and he is kissing her. She is wearing a diaphanous evening gown ; he, a dinner-jacket. About two months have passed since the preceding scene. The time is after midnight. There is a tray of drinks on the desk behind the sofa. She detaches herself from his arms and moves away to* L.C.

LEONORA (*in a strained voice*).   I must go.

CHRISTIAN (*quietly*).   Must you ?

LEONORA.   Of course.

CHRISTIAN.   Isn't that rather inconsistent ?

LEONORA.   Yes—I suppose it is.

CHRISTIAN.   What's the matter ?

LEONORA.   I didn't mean it to be like this——

CHRISTIAN (*still by the fire*).   Don't go away from me yet.

LEONORA.   I must.   (*She crosses to* C. *and picks up her bag from the sofa.*)

CHRISTIAN.   Do you want to ?

LEONORA (*softly*).   No.   (*She stops and turns.*)

CHRISTIAN.   Come back to my arms, it's cold over here by the fire.

LEONORA (*with her face turned away from him*).   I lied just now when I said I didn't mean it to be like this. (L. *of sofa.*)

CHRISTIAN. Does it matter ?

LEONORA. Yes—it matters dreadfully——

CHRISTIAN (*moving towards her*). My dear——

LEONORA (*with panic in her voice*). Please stay there.

CHRISTIAN (*stopping*). Very well.

LEONORA (*with a rush*). I did mean it to be like this, but—but not quite like this—I mean—it was all a trick —I planned it—the first day I came, you remember, when you snubbed me—I teased you about it at dinner to-night—I made up my mind then to make you fall in love with me—now I wish I hadn't—I feel cheap— I feel frightened—I wish with all my heart I hadn't.

CHRISTIAN (*moves to the desk and pours out a drink—with a smile*). I think it was rather a gay trick. Don't be upset. There's nothing to be upset about. Let's sit down quietly and have a drink. Will you have one ?

LEONORA. No, thank you.

CHRISTIAN (L. *of desk*). Leonora, do come and sit down.

LEONORA. Now you're treating me like a patient. (*She turns away to* L.C. *and takes a cigarette from her bag.*)

CHRISTIAN. Only because you're behaving like one.

LEONORA. I see. (*She laughs suddenly.*)

CHRISTIAN. That's better.

LEONORA. I'd like a match.

CHRISTIAN. Here. (*He lights one for her.*) You're a lovely creature. (*He sits at* R. *end of the sofa.*)

LEONORA. I'm all right outside, but I'm not very pleased with myself inside at the moment. (*She sits on the* L. *arm of the sofa.*)

CHRISTIAN. Pangs of conscience are tiresome, Leonora, they're also exceedingly bad for you.

LEONORA. I'm feeling better now.

CHRISTIAN. I gather that the trick is on again.

LEONORA (*sharply*). That was unkind.

CHRISTIAN. You're very touchy.

LEONORA. What about Barbara ?

CHRISTIAN. She's very well, thank you—I had a letter from her this morning.

LEONORA. Are you in love with her?

CHRISTIAN. What on earth did you say that for?

LEONORA. Are you in love with her?

CHRISTIAN. You're behaving like a patient again.

LEONORA. Are you?

CHRISTIAN. Barbara has nothing to do with this. (*He puts down his glass on the desk behind the sofa.*)

LEONORA (*sitting on the sofa*). You're certainly not in love with me.

CHRISTIAN. You have lovely eyes, but there's a little sadness in them, a little disappointment, I could tell your fortune by your eyes—shall I?

LEONORA. I'd rather you didn't.

CHRISTIAN. And your nose——

LEONORA (*looking away*). I'd rather you didn't mention my nose at all.

CHRISTIAN. It's the most unwise nose I've ever seen.

LEONORA. Do stop.

CHRISTIAN. Then there's your mouth——

LEONORA. I must go——

CHRISTIAN. You'd be astounded if you knew how desperately I want to kiss your mouth—again——

LEONORA. Please, Chris——

CHRISTIAN. You're so foolish, up on your romantic high horse—how often have you ridden it wildly until it went lame and you had to walk home?

LEONORA (*rises, crosses to the fireplace and puts her bag on the cocktail table*). Often enough to teach me never to do it again.

CHRISTIAN. That's what made the sadness in your eyes—you should never have left school, it was a grave mistake.

LEONORA. You win.

CHRISTIAN. Do I?

LEONORA. I knew you would—quite early in the evening I knew.

CHRISTIAN. Has it been a happy evening—for you?

LEONORA. No, not really—rather strained.

CHRISTIAN. Were you really angry—that first time we met?

LEONORA. Yes—I think I was.

CHRISTIAN. I didn't mean to be rude.

LEONORA. You certainly did.

CHRISTIAN. Yes, now I come to think of it, I did.

LEONORA. Why ?

CHRISTIAN. You irritated me, you were so conscious of how absolutely beautiful you looked.

LEONORA. I never thought that.

CHRISTIAN. Your manner demanded attention insistently, like a child banging its spoon on the table, making a clamour—yelling for more——

LEONORA. How horrid that sounds.

CHRISTIAN (*rises, moves* L.). Quite natural though. I expect you've always been spoilt.

LEONORA. No, I haven't.

CHRISTIAN. Have you had many lovers ?

LEONORA (*looking down*). No—-not many.

CHRISTIAN. And the few—whoever they were—did you love them ?

LEONORA. Please don't be quite so—clinical. (*Her back to him.*)

CHRISTIAN (*impulsively*). Forgive me—I wanted to know.

LEONORA. I loved somebody once—very much—never so much before—and never so much since.

CHRISTIAN. I see.

LEONORA (*turning to him again*). I know you think my conscience is tiresome and, considering how obviously I threw myself at you, a trifle ill-timed, but it's there all the same and it's making me uneasy—— Please listen, I'm being really honest now—if you and I had an—an affair—how much would it hurt Barbara ?

CHRISTIAN. I don't know. If she knew, I expect it would upset her a good deal, but it would upset her just as much, if not more, if she thought we wanted to and were denying ourselves on her account. Barbara's that sort of person.

LEONORA. You have been married twelve years.

CHRISTIAN. How naïve you are.

LEONORA.   Do you love her?   You never answered me before.

CHRISTIAN.   Yes, I love her deeply and truly and for ever.

LEONORA (*throws away her cigarette in the fireplace, then crosses* R.).   I see.

CHRISTIAN.   I don't suppose you do, but it doesn't matter.

LEONORA.   It matters a lot.

CHRISTIAN (*moving down*).   What do you want? Truth or lies—reality or pretence?

LEONORA.   How clever of you to know, without looking, what you have in your safe.

CHRISTIAN.   Don't be unkind to me, Leonora.

LEONORA.   It's you who are unkind to me.   (*She sits at* R. *end of the sofa*.)

CHRISTIAN.   Why?   In what way?

LEONORA.   It's my own fault, of course——

CHRISTIAN.   Entirely.

LEONORA.   If you feel that it would make our—our flirtation any more satisfactory, I have some X-ray plates of my teeth.

CHRISTIAN.   You really must not be quarrelsome, Leonora.

LEONORA.   I can't help it, you make me angry—horribly angry—I want to hit out at you.

CHRISTIAN.   Any other impulse at this particular stage of the proceedings would be abnormal.

LEONORA.   You're so superbly sure of yourself, aren't you?

CHRISTIAN (*seriously*).   No, the basis of everything I've ever learned is not being sure—not being sure of anyone or anything in the world—myself least of all—— (*He turns away*.)

LEONORA.   Hand me my bag, it's on the table.

CHRISTIAN.   What for?

LEONORA.   I want to powder my—unwise nose.

CHRISTIAN (*handing it to her*).   Here.

LEONORA.   Thank you.

(*She opens her bag and scrutinizes herself in the glass*

inside it. She puts on some lipstick and powders her nose. CHRISTIAN *watches her.*)

CHRISTIAN.   There's a bit of fluff on the left.

LEONORA.   I can see it.

CHRISTIAN.   You mustn't be ungracious.

LEONORA.   I want to go home now. (*She rises.*)

CHRISTIAN.   I'll take you—there's always a taxi on the rank. (*He moves behind the sofa to pick up her cloak.*)

LEONORA.   Please don't, I'd really rather you didn't.

CHRISTIAN (R. *of her, helping her on with her cloak*). Allow me.   You must be raving mad.

LEONORA.   Why—what do you mean ?

CHRISTIAN.   To imagine—— Oh, what's the use——

(*He suddenly crushes her in his arms and kisses her violently.*)

LEONORA.   Don't — please, Chris — don't—— (*She struggles.*)

CHRISTIAN (*pressing her to him*).   Don't be unkind—I want you—you must know that—it wasn't all a trick—it may have started as a trick, but it isn't that now, is it ?   Is it ?

LEONORA (*breaking away from him, breathlessly*).   Yes —yes it is.

CHRISTIAN.   Liar.   (*He takes her hand.*)   Look at me.

LEONORA (*near tears*).   No.   (*She turns away.*)

CHRISTIAN.   Please.   (*He turns her slowly and looks into her eyes.*)

LEONORA (*in a whisper*).   Well—what's my fortune ?

CHRISTIAN.   You're going to love me a little.

LEONORA (*shaking her head*).   That's not enough.

CHRISTIAN.   Oh, yes—yes—more than enough.

LEONORA.   Are you sure ?

CHRISTIAN.   Oh, my dear—my dear——

(*She slips into his arms again as the lights fade on the scene.*)

SCENE IV

It is now April, three months having passed since the preceding scene. The time is about five or six a.m.
There is a greyness in the room because dawn is not far away.

BARBARA *is sitting in the chair by the fire smoking a cigarette. She is wearing a dressing-gown, and there is an ashtray by her side almost filled with cigarette-ends. She shivers slightly, then gets up, draws the curtains back, and pours herself a brandy and soda ; she returns to her chair and then her attention is caught by the sound of the front door opening softly. She closes her eyes for an instant and bites her lip as though she were trying to gather courage, puts down her brandy at the sound of the door.*

CHRISTIAN *comes quietly in from the* R., *he is wearing a light overcoat and hat. His face is tired and strained. He puts on the lights.*

BARBARA (*in as ordinary a voice as she can manage*). Hallo, darling !

CHRISTIAN (*startled*). Barbara !

BARBARA. I'm sorry if I made you jump.

CHRISTIAN. What on earth—— ?

BARBARA. I couldn't sleep.

CHRISTIAN. Oh, I see——

BARBARA. Not all the lights, Chris, it's so glarey.

CHRISTIAN (*switching off the lights*). That better ?

BARBARA. Would you like a drink ?

CHRISTIAN. No—no, thanks. (*He crosses to the fire.*)

BARBARA. I'm having one—it's—it's a bit chilly.

CHRISTIAN (*in a flat voice*). I'm awfully sorry, darling. (*His back to the fire.*)

BARBARA. There isn't anything to be sorry for—I mean this isn't a scene—really it isn't, only I do want to talk to you. I've wanted to for a long while.

CHRISTIAN. I know.

BARBARA. It's probably a bad moment, but—but

during the day it's difficult—there never seems to be any time——

CHRISTIAN.   I meant it when I said I was sorry—I am —desperately sorry.

BARBARA.   Of course you are.   Don't be silly—I know that—it's all beastly—I'm sorry, too ; I'm sorry for you and me and—I'm even sorry for Leonora—— (*She gives a little laugh.*)

CHRISTIAN (*noticing the ashtray*).   Have you smoked all those to-night ?

BARBARA.   Yes—it looks awfully unattractive, doesn't it—like after a party——

CHRISTIAN (*looking away from her, then sitting in the downstage armchair*).   You know about me loving you all the same, don't you—more than anybody in the world ?

BARBARA.   Yes, of course I do, but I'd rather you didn't go on about it just at the moment.   You see, I want so very much not to be emotional.

CHRISTIAN.   Are you very unhappy ?

BARBARA.   Not any more than you, I don't suppose. That's the worst of the whole business, nobody's having a good time.   How is Leonora ?

CHRISTIAN.   She's all right, I've just left her.

BARBARA.   I didn't imagine you'd been to a Masonic dinner, darling.

CHRISTIAN (*smiling wryly*).   No, I didn't think you did.

BARBARA.   I hate her quite normally with all my feminine instincts ; sometimes I get almost violent, all by myself—it's funny, isn't it, after so many years— I've got over wishing to strangle her, though, now ; I just wish she'd never been born.

CHRISTIAN.   I think I do, too.

BARBARA.   I don't see how we can go on like this quite, do you ?   It really is too uncomfortable—that's why I sat up for you.   I'm dreadfully worried ; the personal, loving you part of the affair I could manage, I think—painful as it is—but it's everything else too— we're all in a state, Tim and Susan—I think even Ernest's getting a bit agitated——

(CHRISTIAN *rises and lights himself a cigarette from the table* C.)

(*She laughs again nervously.*) —you're working under such tremendous pressure, and you're so terribly strained and tired—we're all frightened that you'll crack up or something.

CHRISTIAN. Don't worry, I shan't crack up. (*His back to her.*)

(*Pause.*)

BARBARA. Do you want to marry her?

CHRISTIAN. No—it isn't anything to do with marriage.

BARBARA. Does she want you to marry her?

CHRISTIAN. No, I don't think so—no, I'm sure she doesn't.

BARBARA. I can't see why that should make me feel a bit better, but it does.

CHRISTIAN. Oh, Baba—— (*He breaks off miserably.*)

BARBARA (*brightly*). And I'll trouble you not to call me Baba just now, darling—as a psychologist you really ought to know better. (*She rises with her back to the fire.*)

CHRISTIAN (*trying to smile at her*). All right.

BARBARA. I have a plan, you know, otherwise I wouldn't have pounced like this, but before I tell you what it is, I want to know a little more.

CHRISTIAN. Very well, fire away.

BARBARA. First of all, how clearly do you see the situation—in your more detached moments, I mean?

CHRISTIAN. Quite clearly, but my detached moments are getting rarer, I'm afraid.

BARBARA. Can you be detached now?

CHRISTIAN. I'm trying with all my might. (*He sits on the L. arm of the sofa.*)

BARBARA (*turns to him*). Don't worry about me, please don't! I can tread water indefinitely—it would be different if I were still in love with you, but I'm not, any more than you are with me; that was all settled years ago. We are tremendously necessary to each other, though, and I hope to God we always shall be, and I want to know—I want to know—— (*Her voice breaks.*)

CHRISTIAN. How long ?

BARBARA (*with control*). Yes.

CHRISTIAN. I'm submerged now—I can't tell.

BARBARA. Very well then, you must go away. (*She crosses to* R. *end of the sofa.*)

CHRISTIAN. Go away ! How can I ?

BARBARA. You must.

CHRISTIAN. I've thought of it. I wanted to, but it's quite impossible. Also, even if I could, even if there wasn't work or anything to prevent me, it wouldn't be any use—running away never is any use.

BARBARA (*sits at* R. *end of the sofa*). I didn't mean you to go away alone, it's too late for that now. I meant you to go away with her—take two months, three months if necessary—go to the most lovely beautiful place you can think of—relax utterly—give yourself up to loving her without any sense of strain or responsibility —don't think about work or me or any of the things that are standing in the way——

CHRISTIAN (*rising*). I can't, Baba, you know I can't. (*He crosses and sits on the arm of the chair down* L.)

BARBARA. I don't know anything of the sort. It's clear, cold sense. I'm not being noble and self-sacrificing and thinking only of your happiness. I'm thinking of my own happiness too, and, more important still, of your job—you can't deal wisely and successfully with twisted nerve-strained people if you're twisted and nerve-strained yourself. You must see that. It isn't your passion for Leonora alone that's undermining you, it's the fight you're putting up ; you're being torn in half——

CHRISTIAN. Darling, you're making me so dreadfully ashamed.

BARBARA. That's idiotic—unreasonable and idiotic. You said just now that you were submerged—that's true, you are ; you've crushed down your emotions for years, and now you're paying for it. It's nothing to be ashamed of ; with your sort of temperament it

was inevitable—it had to happen, I've been waiting
for it.

CHRISTIAN. Baba !

BARBARA. Let me go on. I'm not submerged, I'm
seeing the whole thing clearly—unless you put a stop
to this agonizing battle between your emotions and your
intelligence, you'll break completely.

(CHRISTIAN *rises and puts out his cigarette.*)

CHRISTIAN (*tortured*). How can I put a stop to it ?
It's there—it's there all the time—every moment of the
day and night—it started easily, so gaily—little more
than a joke ; there were no danger signals whatever.
Then suddenly I felt myself being swept away and I
started to struggle, but the tide was stronger than I
knew ; now I'm far from the land, darling—(*he sits
on the sofa*)—far from my life and you and safety—
I'm struggling still, but the water's terribly deep and
I'm frightened—I'm frightened. (*He moves close to her
and puts his head down on her shoulder.*)

BARBARA (*gently*). I know—I really do know——

CHRISTIAN. It isn't Leonora, it's nothing to do with
Leonora any more ; it's the thing itself—her face and her
body and her charm make a frame, but the picture's in me,
before my eyes constantly, and I can't get it out——

BARBARA. Stop struggling.

CHRISTIAN (*patting her hand*). I can't ! If I stop
struggling I shall be lost for ever. If I didn't know all
the processes it would be easier, but I do—I watch
myself all the time—when I'm talking to patients—in
case I make a slip ; it's as much as I can do sometimes
to prevent myself from suddenly shrieking in their faces
—" Why are you here ? What do you come to me for ?
How can I help you when there's a little brooch between
us—a little brooch with emeralds and sapphires that
someone gave to Leonora years ago—how can I ease
your poor mind when a handsome young man is burnt
to death in a plane—here in the room—he was the
one she really loved, you know, the only one she ever
really loved——"

BARBARA. Oh, my dear—oh, my poor dear !

CHRISTIAN (*with a great effort at control*). Then there's Leonora herself—she's having a hell of a time. The ecstasy's still there—just for a few flaming moments—but in between there are bad hours. You see, I'm finding out things all the time—things about her and things about myself. We're seldom alone together—the ghosts of the people she loved before, or thought she loved, come and join us—they make me sick with jealousy, Baba—me of all people. We can laugh about that one day, can't we ? I ask her questions, you see, because I can't stop myself—and out of her answers the scenes build themselves—and its those dead moments that torture me—then I lose control and say dreadful cruel things to her. I distort her memories for her, dissect them in front of her until they're spoilt and broken into little pieces. Then she cries, not false crying, but real tears for something that's lost . . . and all the time my brain's raising its eyebrows at me and sneering, and then the only thing left is to be sorry—humbly, bitterly sorry—and swear never again to be unkind—never never never again—until the next time—

BARBARA (*quietly*). It's only the strain that makes all that, darling. I wish I could make you see. If only I could get it into your head that there is no reason in the world why you shouldn't love Leonora as much as you want to—for as long as it lasts—you'd be able to give yourself up to it and be happy——

CHRISTIAN. Happy !

BARBARA. You'd probably have quarrels—one always does—but they'd be normal ones, not these dreadful twisted agonies. You must do as I say—it's your only chance. Let Tim take over everything for three months ; he can manage all right with Susan. Wipe me from your mind entirely ; I shall go away somewhere myself. Laura's in Paris, I can go and stay with her, and Mary's taken the Birrels' house in Kent for six months. It's absolutely lovely and I shall be so much happier than I am now, if only I know you're being sensible and giving yourself space.

CHRISTIAN. Space ?

BARBARA. Room to enjoy the best parts of it, without that horrid feeling of hours passing—without the consciousness that there's work to be done the next day and people to see and decisions to make.

CHRISTIAN. It is running away all the same——

BARBARA. What on earth does that matter ? It's being wise that matters. Take the car—don't stop too long in one place, forget everything but just what you're doing at the moment. You really must try it, darling —you see, I've had time to think and you haven't had any time at all.

CHRISTIAN. You don't hate her, do you ?

BARBARA (*suddenly angry*). Good God ! what does it matter if I do ! (*She rises and goes up and round to the back of him.*)

CHRISTIAN. I'm sorry.

BARBARA (*leaning over the back of the sofa*). I'm fighting for you. Leonora's only on the fringe of the business. It's you and me that make my world and the work you've got to do, and the happiness we've had and can have again. My jealousy is not for the desire you have for her, nor for the hours of illusion you buy from her. I'm jealous of the time in between—the waste— those bad hours you told me about just now. I sense futility in all that, and it's that futility that's nagging at you and humiliating you so. Stop trying to balance yourself—come off your tight-rope, it's better to climb down than fall down, isn't it ?

CHRISTIAN. It's bitter, isn't it, to be made to put on rompers again at my age ?

BARBARA. Whether you intended it or not, that remark was definitely funny.

CHRISTIAN. Among other things, I miss not being able to laugh.

BARBARA. That'll all come back.

CHRISTIAN (*rises and crosses* L.). Just at this moment —this now—this immediate moment I'm all right, you know—I expect it's because you're so strong. (*He sits on the arm of the upstage armchair.*)

BARBARA. Well, make the most of it.

CHRISTIAN. You needn't tell me it won't last, I know that.

BARBARA (*crosses to him*). Hang on to it, anyhow, as long as you can, even when you're submerged again, try to remember it.

CHRISTIAN. Have you ever loved anyone else, since me ?

BARBARA. No, I've never happened to want to.

CHRISTIAN. Would you have, if you had wanted to, I mean ?

BARBARA (*lightly*). I expect so.

CHRISTIAN. I wonder how much I should mind.

BARBARA. Do stop whirling about among fictions, there are enough facts to occupy us, God knows. Go away—offer yourself up—get on with it.

CHRISTIAN (*turning*). I don't believe I really love her at all.

BARBARA. This is no moment to go into a technical argument about that, my sweet. Love is a very comprehensive term, you're certainly obsessed, by her, or by yourself through her, and that's quite enough. Oh, dear, it's more than enough——   (*She gives a little laugh.*) Please, Chris——   (*Hands on his shoulders.*)

CHRISTIAN. All right.

BARBARA (*cheerfully*). Well, that's settled—we'll lash Tim into a frenzy of responsibility to-morrow—I mean to-day—you'd better try to get some sleep now.

CHRISTIAN. Yes—I'll try. (*He rises.*)

BARBARA. Good morning, darling——   (*She puts her arms round him, kisses him lightly and goes quickly out of the room R.*)

CHRISTIAN (*as the door closes on her*). Thank you, Baba.

(*The lights fade.*)

SCENE V

Seven months have passed since the preceding scene. It is midnight on the night before the first scene of the play.

When the lights go up on the scene LEONORA *is lying face downwards on the sofa, sobbing.* CHRISTIAN *has his back to the fire.*

CHRISTIAN. For the love of God, stop crying.

(*She continues to sob.*)

I'm sorry—I've said I was sorry——

LEONORA. I can't bear any more.

CHRISTIAN (*coming over to her*). Darling, please——

LEONORA. Don't—don't come near me.

CHRISTIAN (*on one knee by the sofa*). You must forgive me—you must !

LEONORA (*slowly sitting up*). It isn't forgiving—it's that I can't bear any more. I mean it this time—I really can't !

CHRISTIAN (*rises—bitterly*). I should like to know what you propose to do then.

LEONORA (*rises and picks up the cigarette-box from the table* L. *of the sofa*). I'm going—I'm going away for good.

CHRISTIAN. I see.

LEONORA. I'm going now——

CHRISTIAN (*holding her arms*). No, you're not.

LEONORA. Please, Chris——

CHRISTIAN. I was under the impression that you loved me——

LEONORA. Let go of my arms.

CHRISTIAN. More than anyone or anything in the world. How long ago was that you said that to me—how long ago—answer me . . . (*He shakes her.*)

LEONORA (*crying again*). Oh, for God's sake, Chris

——

CHRISTIAN. You love me so much that you have to lie to me—you love me so much that you play tricks on me—you twist me and torture me until I'm driven beyond endurance—then you sob and cry and say I'm cruel.

LEONORA (*frantically*). You're mad—don't look at me like that—you're mad——

CHRISTIAN (*grimly*). Answer me one question, my darling—my dear darling——

LEONORA. Let me go——

CHRISTIAN. Why did you say you hadn't been out to dine with him when you had ?

LEONORA. Because I knew you'd make a dreadful scene about it.

CHRISTIAN. Why didn't you stay the night with him then—you wanted to, didn't you ? What held you back ? Your love for me ! Or was it fear—— ?

LEONORA (*wrenching herself free from him—with cigarette box she crosses to cocktail table where she slams it down.*) Oh, what's the use—what's the use——

CHRISTIAN (*brokenly*). Do you think I like this situation ? You not loving me any more, and me wanting you so——

LEONORA (*turning*). Why do you say that—you've worked it all up in your imagination. None of it's true —none of it's real.

CHRISTIAN. Don't lie any more.

LEONORA. I'm not—I'm not.

CHRISTIAN (*picking up her cloak from the armchair below the fire*). How do I know ? You've lied before— I've caught you out; trivial enough they were, I grant you, but they were lies all the same—little lies or big lies—what's the difference ? Perhaps you forget that charming little episode in Cairo——

LEONORA. Oh, God !

CHRISTIAN. All right—all right. I know I'm dragging things up from the past—why shouldn't I ? After all, the past held portents enough—sign-posts pointing to the present—this present now—this dreary misery.

LEONORA (*sits on the arm of downstage armchair—with a great effort to be calm*). Listen, Chris, I want to go away for a little. I must—I've told you—I really can't bear any more.

CHRISTIAN. You can't bear any more! What about
me?

LEONORA. It's not my fault that you imagine things
and torture yourself.

CHRISTIAN. Tell me one thing—without lying or
evading—tell me one thing honestly——

LEONORA (*wearily*). What is it?

CHRISTIAN. Do you still—love me?

LEONORA. Oh, Chris! (*She turns away hopelessly.*)

CHRISTIAN. Do you?

LEONORA (*rising—tonelessly*). Yes. (*She turns to the
fire.*)

CHRISTIAN. As much as you did in the beginning?

LEONORA. Differently, Chris, things have changed—
a year has gone by since the beginning.

CHRISTIAN. That's an evasion.

LEONORA. It's the truth—nothing stays the same.

CHRISTIAN. You wanted me in the beginning, didn't
you? Whenever I came near you—whenever I touched
you—it was more important than anything in the world,
wasn't it?

LEONORA. Yes—it was.

CHRISTIAN. And now it isn't any more?

LEONORA. Chris—what's the use of——

CHRISTIAN. Answer me! Do you love me as much
as you did in the beginning?

LEONORA (*violently*). No—no—no!

CHRISTIAN. At last!

LEONORA. That's what you wanted, isn't it?—the
truth—that's the truth!

CHRISTIAN. Then you have been lying—for weeks—
for months probably——

LEONORA. Yes, I have—I have.

CHRISTIAN. When did it die, this poor shabby love
of yours?

LEONORA (*wildly*). A long while ago—you killed it
yourself with your insane jealousies and cruelties. You
never trusted me—never for a minute—you've spoiled
hours that could have been perfect by making scenes
out of nothing. You've dug up things that were once

dear to me and made them look cheap and horrible. I can't even go back into my own memory now without finding you there jeering on every threshold—walking with me through the empty rooms—making them tawdry —shutting them off from me for ever. I hate you for that bitterly. (*She turns to the fire.*)

CHRISTIAN. Sentiment for the dead at the expense of the living—very interesting—quite magnificent !

LEONORA. The dead at least have the sense to be quiet.

CHRISTIAN. Long live the dead !

LEONORA (*with bitterness*). You are one of them now.

(*There is a dreadful silence for a moment. They stand quite still looking at each other.*)

CHRISTIAN (*quietly*). Did you mean that ?

LEONORA (*hesitantly*). Yes—I think I did.

CHRISTIAN (*up to her*). Oh—please—please don't mean that !

LEONORA. Let me go away now.

CHRISTIAN. Couldn't you wait another minute ?

LEONORA. It isn't any use—you know it isn't.

CHRISTIAN. Very well.

LEONORA. Good-bye, Chris.

CHRISTIAN. I love you, my darling.

LEONORA. No, it's not love, it hasn't anything to do with love.

CHRISTIAN. I know it's over now—I really do—I won't make any more scenes. I promise.

LEONORA. Good-bye. (*She grips his hand.*)

(CHRISTIAN *crushes her in his arms.*)

CHRISTIAN (*hoarsely*). Is it quite dead—quite dead ?

LEONORA (*struggling*). Don't, Chris—please !

CHRISTIAN. All passion spent—everything tidied up and put back in the box.

LEONORA. Let me go.

CHRISTIAN. The last time I shall kiss you—the last time I shall feel you in my arms—the very last time of all——

LEONORA (*trying to twist away from him*).   Chris——
CHRISTIAN.   Stay still !
LEONORA.   Let me go !
CHRISTIAN.   God damn you, stay still !

(*He kisses her again violently and throws her away from him.   She staggers and falls on to the downstage armchair.*)

How does it feel to be so desirable—to be wanted so much—tell me, please—I want to know—I want to know what your heart's doing now, your loving female heart !   How enviable to be able to walk away into the future, free of love, free of longing, a new life before you and the dead behind you—not quite the dead, though, let's say the dying—the dying aren't as sensibly quiet as the dead—they can't help crying a little—you must walk swiftly out of earshot and don't—don't, I implore you, look back, it would make too dreary a picture for your neat, sentimental memory book.   There's little charm in dying—it's only clinically interesting—the process of defeat, but your viewpoint is far from clinical, my dear—you're a sane, thrilling animal without complications, and the fact that my life has been broken on your loveliness isn't your fault.   I don't believe it's even mine—it's an act of God, darling, like fire and wind and pestilence.   You're in on a grand tragedy, the best tragedy of all, and the best joke, the triumphant, inevitable defeat of mind by matter !   Just for a minute I'm seeing it all clearly, myself and you and the world around us—but it's only a last flare, like a Verey light shooting through the sky, it'll splutter out in a second, leaving everything darker than before, for me too dark to bear.   You see, I had a life to live and work to do and people to love, and now I haven't any more.   They're eager to help, those people I loved and who love me.   I can see them still, gentle and wise and understanding, trying to get to me, straining to clutch my hand, but it's too late—they can't reach me . . .   Get up and go—it doesn't matter any more to me whether you're here or in the moon.

(*During the above speech,* LEONORA *rises, crosses, picks up her bag and exits, leaving the door open. The front door bangs off. He talks as if she were still there. He talks up stage, talks sitting on the sofa. He rises. You see, he intends suicide. He closes the door, draws the curtains back, opens the windows and looks out. He pours himself a stiff drink, gulps it, goes to the mirror, looks at himself, smacks his face. He looks once round the room, puts his hand over his eyes and dashes to the windows.*)

(*Quick Fade.*)

SCENE VI

This scene is the continuation of Scene I.

BARBARA, TIM *and* SUSAN *are in the same places, and* ERNEST *is standing by the door.*

ERNEST (*announcing*). Mrs. Vail.

(LEONORA *comes in. Her eyes are red from crying. She is obviously trying with all her will to control herself.*)

BARBARA. Leonora—— (*She takes her hand.*) I'm so glad you came—— He asked for you.
TIM (*brusquely*). You'd better go in—at once.
BARBARA. Here, drink this—— (*She hands her her cocktail.*) It's important that you don't break down.
LEONORA. I'll be all right.
BARBARA. Please drink it.
LEONORA. Very well. (*She gulps it down.*)
BARBARA. Tim, will you please take her——
TIM. Come this way, will you ?

(TIM *goes to the doors up* L. *and holds one open for*

LEONORA. *She says* " Thank you " *huskily as she goes through.* TIM *follows her and returns in a moment.*)

BARBARA. It wasn't so foggy.

SUSAN. What ?

BARBARA (*crossing up* C.). Last year, I mean, when she came for the first time—it wasn't so foggy.

SUSAN. No—I remember—it wasn't.

(BARBARA *wanders about the room. Down* L., *up* C. *and down* R.)

BARBARA. I wish—I do wish this hadn't had to happen too.

TIM (*gently*). Do sit down, my dear. (*He is by the fire once more.*)

BARBARA. No—I'm all right—I like wandering. (*She moves up and down,* R. *of sofa.*)

TIM (*at cocktail-shaker*). Do you want some more, Susan ?

SUSAN. No, thank you.

BARBARA (*with a tremulous smile*). It's too much of a good thing—it really is—— (*She sits at* R. *end of the sofa, breaks off and turns her head away.*)

(TIM *and* SUSAN *look at her miserably. She recovers herself quickly.*)

I have a dreadful feeling that I'm making it all much horrider for you——

TIM. Don't be so foolish !

BARBARA. I know what I mean, though—I'm behaving well, almost consciously well ; that's always much more agonizing for other people. Don't you think ?

SUSAN. No, it isn't—it's ever so much better.

BARBARA (*blowing her nose*). I'm not at all sure. If I broke down, collapsed completely, there'd be something to do—something for us all to do—smelling salts and brandy and all that.

TIM. Burnt feathers.

BARBARA. Yes, burnt feathers. (*She gives a polite little laugh.*)

Susan (*looking at the door*). I wonder——

Tim (*quickly*). Don't wonder anything—it's better not.

Barbara. You mustn't snap at Susan, Tim, it's beastly of you.

Tim. Sorry, Susan, I didn't mean to snap.

Susan (*trying to smile at him*). I didn't even hear——

Barbara (*suddenly*). I wish she'd come out now—I wish to God she'd come out now.

Tim. She will—in a minute——

(*They wait in silence. Presently* Leonora *comes quietly back into the room.*)

Barbara. Is he ? Is he—— ?

Leonora (R. *of the chair above the fire*). Yes.

Barbara. Oh—oh, dear——   (*She sinks back again on to the sofa.*)

Leonora. He didn't know me ; he thought I was you ; he said—" Baba—I'm not submerged any more—" and then he said " Baba " again—and then—then he died.

(Leonora *goes out of the room*, R., *as the* Curtain *falls.*)

PROPERTY PLOT

SCENE I

Large carpet covering stage.
Lace curtains to windows.
Practical dark red curtains and valance on pelmet-board.
Framed print down stage (over chair 5).
Framed print down stage (over table 10).
Small picture gilt frame (over chair 12).
Large mirror over mantelpeice.
Hunting print on backing, L.
Gilt-frame picture of girl on backing, R.

1. Window-seat with long red cushion.
2. Desk, blotting-pad, brass inkstand, pen, pencil, 3 medical books, small green ashtray, smelling-salts bottle, papers, black telephone, engagement pad, large silver cigarette-box, box of matches, small glass club match-stand.
3. Large leather couch with dark chintz cover, 2 dark red cushions.
4. Chippendale armchair.
5. Chippendale chair.
6. Cabinet with bronze figure on top.
   Inside.—Large pink shell, 2 Scotch china figures, silver glass vase, blue glass vase, 2 blue and white bowls, 2 pink vases, blue and white jug vase.
7. Low coffee table with large glass match-stand, green leaf ashtray, brass cigarette-box, crystal vase of zinnias, box of matches.
8. Table (3 drawers) with Green Dragon, amber glass vase of zinnias, green leaf ashtray, box of matches.
9. Large upholstered armchair with cover.
10. Round bookcase table with glass ashtray, box of matches.
11. Helmet coal-scuttle.
12. Smaller upholstered armchair with cover, round cushion.
13. Steel fender and 3 fire-irons. 3-ply hearth.
14. White mantelpiece with black oxen, small jug vase, photo in frame, 2 vases on black wood pedestals, 2 Deer ornaments.
15. Consul table (6 legs).

Off stage R.—Large silver salver with cocktail-shaker (half full), 5 cocktail glasses (3 filled).

Scene II

Strike vase of flowers off table 8, replace with pot of red flowers.
Strike flowers off table 7, replace with basket bowl of hyacinths,
strike 2 cocktail glasses off desk. Set papers on couch 3.
Curtains open.

Off R.—Silver salver with cocktail-shaker, 5 cocktail glasses,
Bible on small salver.

Scene III

Strike vases of flowers off tables 7 and 8.
Set glass vase of tufted lilies on 7.
Set glass bowl of camellias on 8.
Strike tray with cocktail-shaker and all cocktail glasses.
Set salver with decanter of whisky, syphon of soda, 2 tumblers
on L. of desk 2.
Curtains closed.

Scene IV

Strike vases off tables 7 and 8.
Set glass vase of hydrangeas on 8.
Set blue china bowl of nasturtiums on 7.
Replace dirty glass with clean one.
Fill ashtray on table 10 with cigarette-ends.
Strike burning cigarette from fireplace.
Stand by door slam.

Scene V

Strike hydrangeas, replace with white lilies.
Strike cigarette-ends and dirty glass off table 10.
Set clean glass on salver (desk 2).
(Dresser strikes coat and hat chair, R.)
Stand by door slam—close curtains.

Scene VI

Strike vases of flowers off 7 and 8.
Strike salver with decanter, syphon and glasses off desk **2**.
Move cigarette-box from 10 back to 7.
Reset flowers, as Scene 1.
Set cocktail tray and 3 glasses on **10**.
Set 2 cocktail glasses on desk 2.
Curtains draped open.
Windows closed.

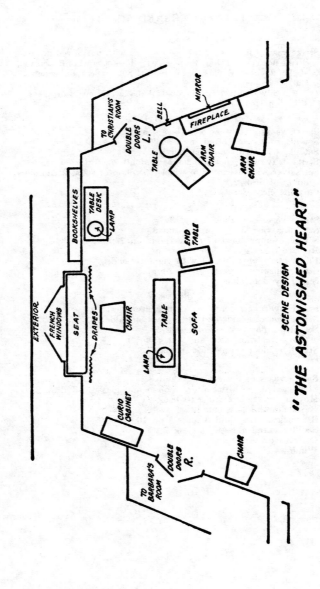

SCENE DESIGN

"THE ASTONISHED HEART"

Other Publications for Your Interest

VIVIEN
(COMIC DRAMA)

By PERCY GRANGER

2 men, 1 woman—Unit set

Recently staged to acclaim at Lincoln Center, this lovely piece is about a young stage director who visits his long-lost father in a nursing home and takes him to see a production of "The Seagull" that he staged. Along the way, each reveals a substantial truth about himself, and the journey eventually reaches its zenith in a restaurant after the performance. "A revealing father-son portrait that gives additional certification to the author's position as a very original playwright."—N.Y. Times. "The dialogue has the accuracy of real people talking."—N.Y. Post.

LANDSCAPE WITH WAITRESS
(COMEDY)

By ROBERT PINE

1 man, 1 woman—Interior

Arthur Granger is an unsuccessful novelist who lives a Walter Mitty-like fantasy existence. Tonight, he is dining out in an Italian restaurant which seems to have only one waitress and one customer—himself. As Arthur selects his dinner he has fantasies of romantic conquest, which he confides to the audience and to his notebook. While Arthur's fantasies take him into far-fetched plots, the waitress acts out the various characters in his fantasy. Soon, Arthur is chattering and dreaming away at such a quick clip that neither he nor we can be entirely sure of his sanity. Arthur finishes his dinner and goes home, ending as he began—as a lover *manqué*. " . . . a landscape of the mind."—Other Stages. " . . . has moments of true originality and a bizarre sense of humor . . . a devious and slightly demented half-hour of comedy."—N.Y. Times. Recently a hit at New York's excellent Ensemble Studio Theatre.

Other Publications for Your Interest

A GALWAY GIRL
(ALL GROUPS—DRAMA)
By GERALDINE ARON

1 man, 1 woman—Interior

A married couple, seated at opposite ends of a table, reminisce about their life together. Each presents the situation from his or her point of view, rarely addressing each other directly. The characters are young to begin with, then middle-aged, then old, then one of them dies. The anecdotes they relate are both humorous and tragic. Their lives seem wasted, yet at the end the wife's muted gesture of affection conveys the love that can endure through years of household bickering and incompatibility. A critical success in London, Ireland and the author's native South Africa. "A very remarkable play."—Times Literary Supplement, London. "A touching account of two wasted lives."—Daily Telegraph, London. "A minute tapestry cross-stitched with rich detail—invested with a strong strain of uncomfortable truths."—The Irish Times, Dublin.

TWO PART HARMONY
(PLAY)
By KATHARINE LONG

1 man, 1 woman—Interior

A play about a confrontation of wits between an alert, pre-adolescent girl and a mentally unsettled child-man. On a spring morning in 1959, eight year old Jessie Corington, home alone on a sick day from school, receives an unexpected visit from Hank Everett, a former friend of the family who used to look like Bobby Darin. From the moment he arrives, Hank's eccentric behavior challenges Jessie's cherished belief in adult maturity. Gradually, however, she welcomes her new found playmate and becomes entranced as he enlists her aid in a telephone search for his estranged wife. As the play builds, their bond of friendship is almost shattered when the violence beneath Hank's innocence surfaces against his will. "The work of an artist skilled in deft, understated draughtmanship."—Village Voice.